Dear Parents:

Congratulations! Your child is taking the first steps on an exciting journey. The destination? Independent reading!

STEP INTO READING® will help your child get there. The program offers five steps to reading success. Each step includes fun stories and colorful art or photographs. In addition to original fiction and books with favorite characters, there are Step into Reading Non-Fiction Readers, Phonics Readers and Boxed Sets, Sticker Readers, and Comic Readers—a complete literacy program with something to interest every child.

Learning to Read, Step by Step!

Ready to Read   Preschool–Kindergarten
• big type and easy words • rhyme and rhythm • picture clues
For children who know the alphabet and are eager to begin reading.

Reading with Help   Preschool–Grade 1
• basic vocabulary • short sentences • simple stories
For children who recognize familiar words and sound out new words with help.

Reading on Your Own   Grades 1–3
• engaging characters • easy-to-follow plots • popular topics
For children who are ready to read on their own.

Reading Paragraphs   Grades 2–3
• challenging vocabulary • short paragraphs • exciting stories
For newly independent readers who read simple sentences with confidence.

Ready for Chapters   Grades 2–4
• chapters • longer paragraphs • full-color art
For children who want to take the plunge into chapter books but still like colorful pictures.

STEP INTO READING® is designed to give every child a successful reading experience. The grade levels are only guides; children will progress through the steps at their own speed, developing confidence in their reading. The F&P Text Level on the back cover serves as another tool to help you choose the right book for your child.

Remember, a lifetime love of reading starts with a single step!

Copyright © 2019 by Penguin Random House LLC

All rights reserved. Published in the United States by Random House Children's Books, a
division of Penguin Random House LLC, New York. Originally published in hardcover and trade
paperback in the United States by Penguin Young Readers, an imprint of Penguin Random House
LLC, New York, in 2019.

Step into Reading, Random House, and the Random House colophon are registered trademarks of
Penguin Random House LLC.

Visit us on the Web!
StepIntoReading.com
rhcbooks.com

Educators and librarians, for a variety of teaching tools, visit us at
RHTeachersLibrarians.com

Library of Congress Cataloging-in-Publication Data is available upon request
ISBN 978-0-593-43226-6 (trade) — ISBN 978-0-593-43227-3 (lib. bdg.)

Printed in the United States of America
10 9 8 7 6 5 4 3 2 1

This book has been officially leveled by using the F&P Text Level Gradient™ Leveling System.

CORDUROY'S Hike

by Alison Inches
illustrated by Allan Eitzen
based on the characters created by Don Freeman

Random House 🏠 New York

Lisa checked her backpack.

Peanut butter sandwich.

Juice. Hat. Jacket.

"You have to stay here, Corduroy,"

Lisa said.

"You might get lost on a hike."

I will not get lost, thought Corduroy.

He crawled into the backpack.

I will be safe in here.

Beep! Beep! The bus had come.

Lisa sat next to Susan.

"What did you bring?" asked Susan.

Lisa opened her backpack.

"A peanut butter sandwich.

Juice. And *Corduroy!*

How did you get in here?

You might get lost on a hike."

"He will be safe in your backpack,"
said Susan.

Lisa hoped Susan was right.

At the park,

Lisa and Susan found a stream

with a bridge over it.

They dropped sticks into the water.

Then they ran across the bridge.

The sticks came out the other side.

"I see mine!" they cried.

Then it was time to hike.

Off they went.

Bounce! Bounce! Bounce!

Corduroy bounced along

in the backpack.

The class hiked higher and higher.

"I can see a farm!" said Susan.

"I can see a church!" said Lisa.

I can't see a thing, thought Corduroy.

11

Corduroy poked his head out.

That's better, thought Corduroy.

Now I can see, too.

Bounce! Bounce! Bounce!

Corduroy bounced along

in the backpack.

This is fun, thought Corduroy.

Look, no hands!

Whoops!

Corduroy bounced out

of the backpack . . .

Thud!

. . . and onto the trail.

Lisa will pick me up, he thought.

But Lisa did not pick him up.

Lisa will come back for me.

But Lisa did not come back.

Soon two hikers came by.

They picked up Corduroy.

"You must have an owner,"

said one hiker.

She set Corduroy on a branch.

"Your owner will see you

up here," she said.

Corduroy waited for Lisa.

He sang songs.

He watched the birds.

Then he saw a Cub Scout troop

hiking up the trail.

"Look!" said a Cub Scout. "A bear!"

The Cub Scout picked up Corduroy

and tossed him in the air.

Then he tossed him to another boy.

They tossed Corduroy

back and forth.

Corduroy felt like a football.

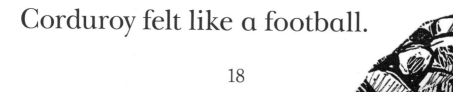

Another boy ran ahead.

Corduroy flew through the air.

They did it again.

And again.

And again.

Then, *thud!*

Corduroy landed on

the side of the trail.

The Cub Scouts walked on.

Corduroy tried to stand up.

He felt dizzy.

He tipped to one side.

22

He tipped to the other.

Then Corduroy tipped over.

Splash!

Oh my! thought Corduroy.

The water took Corduroy away.

It took him over rocks

and under a bridge . . .

Then, *zoom!*

Corduroy zoomed over a waterfall.

He zoomed under another bridge.

Bonk!

He stopped on a rock.

Oh dear, thought Corduroy.

I think I am stuck.

And I am cold.

And wet.

And more lost.

Soon it began to get dark.

The class came back

down the trail.

Lisa sat down.

Corduroy was gone.

She had looked everywhere for him.

The teacher clapped her hands.

"Time to get on the bus!"

Lisa sat next to the window.

Susan sat beside her.

"I was playing the stick
game again," she said.
"My sticks all came out
on the other side."
Lisa nodded.

"Something else came out
on the other side, too," said Susan.

"Corduroy!" cried Lisa.

"I'm so glad I've got you."

Me too, thought Corduroy.